SITTING TARGET

Titles in Teen Reads:

Copy Cat TOMMY DONBAVAND	**Fair Game** ALAN DURANT	**Mama Barkfingers** CAVAN SCOTT
Dead Scared TOMMY DONBAVAND	**Jigsaw Lady** TONY LEE	**Pest Control** CAVAN SCOTT
Just Bite TOMMY DONBAVAND	**Mister Scratch** TONY LEE	**The Hunted** CAVAN SCOTT
Home TOMMY DONBAVAND	**Stalker** TONY LEE	**The Changeling** CAVAN SCOTT
Kidnap TOMMY DONBAVAND	**Dawn of the Daves** TIM COLLINS	**Nightmare** ANN EVANS
Ward 13 TOMMY DONBAVAND	**Joke Shop** TIM COLLINS	**Sitting Target** JOHN TOWNSEND
Deadly Mission MARK WRIGHT	**The Locals** TIM COLLINS	**Snow White, Black Heart** JACQUELINE RAYNER
Ghost Bell MARK WRIGHT	**Troll** TIM COLLINS	**The Wishing Doll** BEVERLY SANFORD
The Corridor MARK WRIGHT	**Insectoids** ROGER HURN	**Underworld** SIMON CHESHIRE
Death Road JON MAYHEW	**Billy Button** CAVAN SCOTT	**World Without Words** JONNY ZUCKER

Badger Publishing Limited, Oldmedow Road, Hardwick Industrial Estate, King's Lynn PE30 4JJ
Telephone: 01553 816083

www.badgerlearning.co.uk

SITTING TARGET

JOHN TOWNSEND

Sitting Target ISBN 978-1-78147-565-2

Text © John Townsend 2014
Complete work © Badger Publishing Limited 2014

All rights reserved. No part of this publication may be
reproduced, stored in any form or by any means mechanical,
electronic, recording or otherwise without the prior permission
of the publisher.

The right of John Townsend to be identified as author of this Work has
been asserted by him in accordance with the Copyright, Designs and
Patents Act 1988.

Designer: Bigtop Design Ltd
Cover Image: Shutterstock/Adam Wasilewski

Lee lives with his mum in a quiet street. Too quiet. When a stranger breaks in, Lee is suddenly thrown into the secret and disturbing world of international espionage. Now he has a scary job to do in a frantic race against time. He might only be fourteen and in a wheelchair, but he's sure of one thing – he must never become a sitting target. Not now *they* are after him…

CHAPTER 1

HOME ALONE

Lee first saw the face through the front door. A nose pressed against the frosted glass.
A steamy smear spread from the lips. Dark eyes peered in. Blinking. Staring. Scary.

Lee threw himself on the floor and lay still. His heart was thumping like mad. No one ever called at their house. Mum always told him not to answer the door to strangers. He'd never felt so scared. Not in his own home. He just hoped the eyes hadn't seen him.

Being alone had never been a problem before. Lee was used to it. Until now. He'd always liked being in the house on his own. It was the only time he could do what he liked. No one to nag or fuss. But all of a sudden it felt different. Who could he call for help? No one was next door – they were away. It was already getting dark.

The phone was just out of reach. Lee grabbed a leg of the wobbly hall table. It shook and crashed down on him. The phone, note pad, pens and a pot plant fell on top of him. As he lay at the foot of the stairs, he wished he hadn't snapped at his mum at breakfast.

"Of course I'll be all right here by myself. I'm fourteen. I like being on my own. Why do you treat me like a helpless zombie?"

But now he couldn't manage – and he knew it.

There was nothing Lee could do. The dark shape through the glass was pushing a key in the lock. It jangled and clicked as Lee pulled himself across the floor towards the door. He'd try to fix the chain before the door could open. He might even reach the catch on the lock. That would stop the man getting in. That's if Lee's legs didn't give way. But he didn't have time to find out. Just as he crawled to the door, it opened and pushed towards him with a thud.

Lee fell back and stared up at a man standing over him. The door slammed shut, followed by a scary silence. They were alone in the house. Both sweating and breathless, they stared into each other's eyes.

It was Lee who spoke first. He was surprised at how calm he managed to sound.

"Before you kill me, there's something you should know." He held up his phone.

"I've filmed you breaking in. I've just sent it to my mum's phone. The police will know who you are from your eyes. They can read them like fingerprints. So now you know."

The man stood very still for a few seconds. He seemed lost for words. Slowly he pulled the hood from his head and took off his gloves. He knelt down beside Lee and held out his hand. "I'm really sorry," he said softly. "I'm sorry you fell. I'm sorry I broke in. I'm sorry I scared you. But it was the only way. You are a brave boy."

Lee's heart was still thumping. He tried to make sense of this man with jet-black hair and staring brown eyes. Quite young – with a soft voice – foreign.

"We haven't got anything," Lee told him. "There's no money in the house. Mum doesn't get paid much and I haven't got a dad living here. I've only got a few quid in a tin upstairs. You can have it. But if you must rob us, don't smash things up. Please. Mum gets upset and stressed. She hasn't been well, you see, and…"

The man put a finger to his lips. "Shhh. I am not here to hurt you. I am not a robber. I'm a friend. I want you to be my friend."

Lee tried to pull away and shuffle into the kitchen. *This man's a nut case,* he thought. *He's broken into our house just to ask me to be his friend. How weird is that?*

The man read his mind. "Don't worry, I'm not mad. And I'm not a killer. If you can help me, I will pay you." He took a wad of £20 notes from his pocket. "Have this to begin with."

"Mum's told me never to take money from strangers. Even scary ones who break in."

For the first time the man smiled. "You're a bright kid. I knew you were. I've been watching you for a few days. I could tell you have a lot of spark."

"Watching me?" Lee moved his hand to the phone under his leg. He'd try to call the police. "Where have you been watching me?" His finger pressed 9 on the keypad.

"At the clinic."

"I go there a lot." Lee tried to keep the man talking while his finger pressed two more 9s. "I'm still having physio. I was born with something called CP. As I grow, I have to have my legs twisted. I had a big operation this year. They broke the bones and re-set them. I want to be walking on my sticks by next year. Till then I have to use the wheelchair. I like being at home as I can crawl around as much as I like. At least, I used to like being at home…"

"I'm sorry. I did knock on your back door. I knew you were in. I must talk to you. Alone." The man put his hand on Lee's arm. "I know what you are doing. I can't blame you. Go ahead and call the police. I won't stop you. It's just that I thought you might be able to help. Maybe I was wrong. But you're the only one who can save us. I'm desperate. I'll pay you all I've got. I'll do anything."

Lee lifted the phone. He paused as the voice on the other end asked for his details.

"Are you still there?" it asked.

"Yes," he said softly. He looked up at the man's face. A worried face, with pleading brown eyes. Eyes with tears in them. Lee stared at them as he calmly whispered into the phone. "It's OK, thanks. I think I'm all right now."

He slowly put down the phone.

CHAPTER 2

THE DEAL

The kettle boiled as Lee poured milk into two mugs.

"I can't believe I'm doing this," he said. "Mum will go mad if she ever finds out. A minute ago you were breaking into our house and scaring me to death. And now I'm making you a cup of tea. This is crazy. Biscuit?"

"Thanks. Can I help?" The stranger stood by the sink, watching.

Lee turned on his kitchen stool and gave him a stare. "Don't go there. It might not be the best cup of tea you've ever had, but I can do it by myself. I didn't tell the police to come just now because I felt sorry for you. It was a great change from the other way round. All my life people have looked at me with pity. But you didn't treat me like I was a helpless kid who couldn't walk. You were different. You're the first person who's ever asked me to help them. It felt good. That's what I've been waiting for. The chance to show I can cope."

The man smiled. "You can cope all right. You've got guts. I like you, Lee."

"You know my name?"

"Sure. I've checked you out. Call me Alex. I won't tell you my full name. It's too long." He looked up at the clock on the kitchen wall.

"Don't worry," Lee said. "Mum won't be back yet. She's doing extra hours on the check-out at Tesco's. Anything to pay the gas bill. She's upset about money at the moment. She takes pills for stress." He bit into a Jaffa cake. "Why am I telling you all this? It's none of your business! You're a total stranger. I always talk too much when I'm scared."

"Your secrets are safe with me," Alex said. "I know far too many secrets already." He put his hand on Lee's shoulder. "And there's no need for you to be scared. I'd never harm anyone. Anyway, you've sent your mum my picture, remember?"

Lee paused. "That was a lie. A bluff. It was all I could think to say in the panic. I didn't have time to send it. But I can tell you're not going to kill me now. You don't look like a killer any more." Lee sipped his tea thoughtfully. "I think you're some sort of a spy. I like spy books."

"In a way," Alex said. "After all, I've been spying on you, haven't I? And now I want you to be a sort of spy, too."

"Really? Where?"

"The clinic. The Health Centre where you go. It has a few beds for special patients. One of them is my brother. He's very sick and he's got a police guard. That's why I can't get in to see him. We're not meant to be in this country, you see. I'll be arrested. So I need someone to go in for me. Someone that no one will suspect. Someone who won't get caught getting the secrets. Before it's too late."

Lee looked puzzled. "What sort of secrets?"

"A list of names. Names of men from my country who try to kill us. You see, my brother and I escaped here. We told the truth about our leaders back home. Now they want us killed. My brother was poisoned before he could give me the names of the killers. We need to warn the world about what's going on back home."

Lee was quiet for a while. "Even if I get what you want, how will it do any good?"

"You'll save lives. We must post the truth online.

And, like I said, I'll pay you." He pointed at the £20 notes he'd put by the cooker. "There's £500 there. That's the first half. You get the rest when you succeed."

Lee's eyes widened. "Wow! A grand! Cool. That seems like easy money to me."

"Maybe," Alex said seriously. "But there could be a risk."

"What sort of a risk?"

Alex put down his mug and looked Lee straight in the eyes. "There's a man known as Zeta. He will stop at nothing to kill us. I've never seen him but I'll know him when I do. Part of his ear is missing. It was shot off. Now he'll shoot anyone who gets in his way."

"So, if I help you," Lee said, putting down his mug, "will this Zeta be after me, too?"

"He won't find out. We'll keep it secret." Alex rinsed his mug under the tap. "Let's face it, if he ever did find out about you…" he dried the mug and looked up. "He'd shoot you dead."

CHAPTER 3

THE MISSION

The letterbox rattled. Lee looked up from his breakfast with a start. For the last two days he'd been on edge every time a sound came from the front door. His mum picked up the letters from the doormat.

"I keep finding mud on this carpet," she called to him. "Did you knock my pot plant off the hall table?"

"I fell over, that's all."

He looked back at the TV screen. Just more boring news stories. His mind began to wander.

He wondered when Alex would get in touch with him again. There had been no word from him after he'd left with a, "You'll be hearing from me soon."

Lee had put some of the money away in a tin under his bed. He was due at the clinic in a few hours but he didn't know exactly what Alex wanted him to do.

It was as if Lee's thoughts flashed on the TV screen. There, right in front of him, was Alex's face. Those same eyes were staring at him from the screen. It didn't seem real. Nor did the news reader's voice:

Police say the body found shot dead on a train last night was this man. Details of the murder are still not clear. It seems he was Alexander Kinkova, thought to be on the run....

"Not more shooting. I can't stand all this bad news." Lee's mum switched off the TV and sat beside him. "What are you looking so glum about, love?" She touched his arm.

Lee stared at the blank screen. He didn't move. His mum kept talking. "Cheer up. I'm the one who needs to look gloomy. I've just got this. Another bill. They told me it wouldn't cost much to fix the car. Look at it – £432. There's no way I can afford that. Never."

She put her face in her hands. Lee saw her tears drip onto the table. He hated it when she cried. He wanted to say something but the words wouldn't come. He was still stunned from the news on the TV. It felt as if he was dreaming.

"I've got some money you can have," he said. He was dying to switch the TV back on.

"Not this sort of money, you haven't," she sobbed. "I just don't know what I can do." She pushed two other letters across the table. "I daren't open these. If they're bills as well…"

"Don't worry, Mum." Lee took a quick look to see if they looked like bills. One did. It was in red. A final demand. But the other letter was thicker. Lee looked more closely and was surprised to see his name on it. Without thinking, he slid it off the table into his lap. He somehow knew this was best kept secret.

"I'll get you a cup of coffee, Mum," he said, tucking the letter in his shirt.

"No, love. You finish your breakfast."

Lee wanted to scream. She'd never let him try to help. She always thought he'd fall or make a mess. "I just want to make a difference," he snapped. He, too, felt like crying.

He wheeled himself into the hall to the foot of the stairs and clambered up to his room. As he lay on his bed, he took out the letter and opened the envelope. It was stuffed with £20 notes. Pinned to one of them was a note.

Hi Lee,

I've had to act fast. I'm being followed. Zeta is on to me. If he gets me you must act alone. PLEASE. You will make a real difference. People in my country must be warned about the men on the list. Men with important jobs who cannot be trusted. Most of them are killers.

My brother's name is Georgi. The code is PRO PATRIA. Tell him that and he'll give you the names and an email address to send them to. Then destroy all information. Burn this note. Don't let Zeta get hold of it. Never.

Don't tell the police. Not until the job is done. They will only hold things up. It is urgent. Thank you, Lee. You're a great kid. Sorry I scared you. I would give you more money if I had it. You deserve it. Good luck.

Alex

Lee sat on his bed and counted the money. Over £500. He put it in the tin with the rest and slid it under his bed. There was more than enough to pay all the bills. He looked at his watch. In a few hours he had to be at the clinic. He needed time to think. There were things to do. He read Alex's letter many times.

There was no doubt in Lee's mind. He was going to do this job. This was his chance to prove he could be useful. He wanted to do something for Alex, too. It was strange. Just a few days ago he'd never known about Alex. Now he felt really sad that Alex had been killed. One of the last things he'd done was write to Lee. That made him feel important. For the first time in his life. But he also felt scared. There could be danger in all this.

Lee thought he might need to take a few things on his visit to the clinic. Just in case. He began to get ready for his secret mission. A mission called **PRO PATRIA**. Whatever that might mean. He feared it meant something in particular. Danger.

CHAPTER 4

THE CLINIC

"There's no parking space. We're late!" Lee's mum gripped the steering wheel and swore.

"It's OK, Mum. Just let me out and I'll go in by myself. It's no big deal. You can go shopping. Come back for me in an hour." Lee smiled at her and hoped she'd agree.

"Don't be silly, Lee. I can't leave you on your own. You'll never cope."

He snapped at her with real anger. "Mum, I *want* to go in on my own. It's about time I did things by myself. I'll never learn to cope if you don't give me a chance. Go on, you go."

He took a £5 note from his pocket. "There you are, go and have a nice cup of coffee and a cake. Chill out. See you in an hour." He opened the car door and swung his legs outside. "Just put the chair here for me and I'll do the rest."

They argued until Lee had to use the words he only kept for an emergency. He hated saying it but out they came… "Dad would let me go in on my own. He wants me to grow up and cope for myself."

His Mum looked cross. "Right. Go on, then. Don't blame me if you fall over or get hurt. Don't expect me to come running to pick you up. And take off that silly red baseball cap."

"Anything you say, Mum!" He took off his cap and grinned. It felt good to get his own way for a change. In minutes he was wheeling himself through the clinic doors. He turned to wave at his mum as she drove past… before he pulled the cap back on his head and sped down an alley into the next street. Within minutes he was back and racing through the clinic doors.

"Hi, Lee," the nurse behind the desk called. "No Mum today?"

"No," he grinned. "Left to cope on my own without anyone to hold my hand!"

"You poor little soul! Just park over there for ten minutes and you can go through. The physio's running a bit late."

The nurse smiled and returned to sort out the queue waiting at her desk. Lee thought he'd use the ten minutes to find Georgi's room. He already had a plan for getting past the police guard.

"Are you Lee?" A man in uniform appeared beside him.

"Yes," he said, looking up with surprise. "Is it time to go through already?"

"I've been sent to collect you. The doctor over at our other clinic wants to see you first. It won't take long. I'll pop you over in the ambulance." He winked. "I might try the siren and flashing light if you like! Come on, then." He pushed Lee's chair to the door.

Lee slammed on the brake. "Hold on," he said. "We need to tell the nurse." He waved at her but she was so busy at the desk she didn't see him. The man suddenly let off the brake and shoved him out through the door. They sped down the ramp towards the waiting ambulance as Lee shouted and waved his arms.

"Shut up and do as you're told," the man yelled as he pushed the chair up a ramp into the back of the ambulance. Lee was flung inside and the doors slammed behind him.

"Now, just listen to me. This is soundproof so you can scream and shout as much as you like. No one will hear you. But I want to hear you. You're going to tell me all you know. And just in case you don't do as you're told." … The man took out a syringe, "this needle has enough poison in it to get rid of you for good. In seconds. I hate kids so I'll be pleased to use it. Now tell me what you know about Georgi."

"I've never met anyone called Georgi. And I don't know who you are, either." Lee's hand slipped down the side of his chair. He'd hidden a few things under a cushion. Just in case. It was time to use one of them.

"Never mind who I am. What did Georgi tell you? He's only got ten minutes to live. By two o'clock he'll be dead. Tell me what his brother told you. We know he came to see you. Tell me or you'll feel pain."

The man gripped Lee's neck and leaned forwards so they almost touched noses. Lee could hardly breathe as he looked up at the man's ears. He wasn't the dreaded Zeta, but scary enough. It was time to strike before it was too late.

Lee had come prepared – with a weapon. It was the only thing he could think of – a water pistol filled with vinegar. He'd once seen it in a spy comic. But now it was time to put it to the test. As the hand gripped his neck tighter, Lee's fingers found the trigger. He whipped out the pistol and squirted it straight in the man's eyes.

As the scream burst in his ears, Lee could breathe again – but he had to act fast. Weak though his legs were, he kicked with all his strength. The man fell backwards, still rubbing his eyes and swearing. He cracked his head on a bracket holding a stretcher. He crumpled, groaned and rolled across the ambulance.

Lee dived from his chair and crawled towards the syringe. He didn't want that deadly needle left lying around. He'd get rid of it. But just as he reached it, the man lashed out. Lee fell back against the wheelchair, dropping the syringe onto the seat. That's when the man dived at him. Lee slid behind the wheelchair and pulled himself up. As the man staggered towards him, Lee pushed the chair at him. It crunched into the man's legs and he fell into the chair. Lee scooped him up and slammed the chair at the doors. They burst open and the chair flew out down the ramp.

As the wheelchair hit the ground, it skidded and tipped over. The man shot out, headfirst. He slumped on the path with a thud. But there, sticking out of the man's behind, was the needle. He tried to get up, but began mumbling as if he was drunk. He crawled along the path, pulling the needle out with a growl. Suddenly, he tumbled into a flower bed. In seconds he lay still, his head down in the mud. His groans had stopped.

Lee slid down the ramp, picked up his wheelchair and scooped up his things. He looked down at the dead man in the flowers. Then he looked at his watch. Five to two. He only had five minutes to find Georgi.

Back in his wheelchair, Lee scooted back into the clinic. He edged through the door and past the queue inside. He swept past, heading for the doors marked 'Short Stay Unit'. He didn't look back as he sped towards the swing doors. He knew he had to be quick. Time was running out – fast.

CHAPTER 5

THE TOP FLOOR

The clinic was a maze of corridors. At last Lee came to a flight of stairs with the sign: 'PRIVATE WARDS – top floor'. There was no way he could get up there in time. He'd have to take the lift.

As he skidded into the lift, Lee thumped the button for the top floor and the doors slid shut. It was only then he thought, *What do I do now?* He was about to ask for a list of names from a stranger who was dying. It all seemed hopeless. He'd never get to the room in time. Not if he still had to get past the police guard. And where was the dreaded Zeta?

The lift stopped and the doors opened. Lee raced out into a long corridor full of hospital smells – but no people. The shiny floor and white doorways were empty – apart from a cleaner in green overalls. And at the far end, on a chair by a door, sat a policeman. Lee headed towards him. A doctor in a white coat swept past without taking any notice. That was a good sign. Lee clearly didn't look out of place. A nurse came past with a trolley. "Hello, love," she smiled.

The policeman was reading a book, but he looked up as Lee got closer.

"What can I do for you, young man?"

Lee pulled an envelope from under his cushion. "I've made a card. A 'Get Well' card."

"Really?" the policeman frowned. "Who for?"

Lee looked up at the door. "For the person in room 12."

"Do you know him?"

"I'm doing a project at school. To visit sick people. Can I give it to him?"

"Afraid not, son. No visitors allowed. Give me the card and I'll pass it on."

Lee feared this would happen. He'd have to use the pin in his pocket. He jabbed it into his leg and his eyes watered. "But I've come a long way and I made it all by myself. I just want to cheer him up to help him get better." The tears spilled down his face. "I used to be in that room. After my accident. I know what it's like to be stuck in there with no visitors. Please let me say hello. My teacher is waiting for me downstairs. I won't take long. It'll make my day. Please." He sobbed into a hanky and waited.

The policeman sighed. He peered through the

small window in the door. "He's awake but it's more than my job's worth. I guess it won't hurt. You don't look like an assassin! Just say hello and give him the card. That's all. Be quick. Come straight out again. Is that clear?"

Lee's face lit up. "Thank you!" He pushed through the door, which swung shut behind him.

A man lay propped up in bed. He looked very pale, with dark rings round his eyes. He was young, but totally bald. His eyes were closed as he listened to an iPod. Lee's chair knocked the bed and the man opened his eyes – startled.

Lee whispered, "Your brother Alex told me to come. He told me to say **PRO PATRIA**. I don't know what it means, but…"

The man leaned forwards. "At last. I'm so glad you're here. I just heard on the radio that my brother was killed. We knew it was a risk. **PRO PATRIA** means 'for our country'. You are helping many people back home. The evil men out there tried to kill me. I am sick but I need to send a message fast. You have a phone?"

"Yes." Lee held it out. He was amazed that Georgi didn't look as if he'd die at any minute.

"Please let me use it. The police think I am a bad man who should not be in this country. They do not let me use a phone. Zeta stole my passport and papers. He also stole my hair. It all fell out after he put poison in my food."

He tapped a list of names into the phone.

Lee looked at his watch. It was two o'clock. Why did the man in the ambulance say Georgi would soon be dead? Suddenly, there were voices just outside. Lee turned towards the door. He pulled himself up to look through the glass. The policeman was talking to the cleaner in green overalls. Lee gasped. The lower part of the cleaner's ear was missing.

"It's Zeta! He's out there with a gun."

For an ill man, Georgi moved very fast. "Quick, into the bathroom. Leave your chair. Give me your baseball cap."

Lee threw him the cap as he scrambled through the bathroom door. Georgi stuffed pillows in his bed and another on Lee's chair. Then he threw the red cap on top so it looked from behind as if Lee was still sitting there. Georgi struggled into the bathroom and shut the door. They both sat still, Georgi panting and trying hard not to cough.

Out in the corridor, Zeta had knocked the policeman to the floor with one chop to the neck. He barged into Georgi's room, aimed a pistol and pulled the trigger. Three shots slammed into the bed. One after another. Three holes ripped through the sheets into the pillows underneath. In the next second, Zeta pointed the gun at the back of Lee's chair. He pulled the trigger again – twice. A hole punched through the chair. Another ripped through the baseball cap. As it flew across the room and hit the bathroom door, Zeta turned and ran.

The 'killing' was over in seconds. But the intended victims sat alive and well in the bathroom. Both were stunned and breathless as they slowly emerged from their hideout. Feathers and dust still danced above the bed. Lee picked up his cap, his finger poking through the scorched bullet hole. He turned to Georgi with wide eyes. Still shocked, they shook hands. Only then did they dare to smile.

Georgi held up the phone. "Message sent and received. Success at last! We've done it. All thanks to you."

Lee's face beamed. He wasn't useless after all. He'd made a difference at last.

CHAPTER 6

THE LAST WORD

The policeman crashed into the room. He held his nose as blood dripped through his fingers.

"I need that chair of yours, son," he shouted. "Quick!"

"Yes, of course. I'll get you a nurse," Lee said.

"Not for me. I need wheels. I'm going to get him."

He pulled the chair through the door into the corridor. Pushing it in front of him, he began running. As he gained speed, people in the corridor leapt out of his way. They pressed themselves against the walls. A nurse screamed and ran for cover.

Zeta had already reached the end of the corridor. He'd changed from his overalls and now wore a doctor's white coat. No one stopped to take any notice of him. He walked quickly towards the stairs. Within minutes he'd be out of the building and away. That was his plan. But the policeman had other ideas. He was already hurtling towards the top of the stairs at full speed. So fast that nothing could stop him.

After just a few steps down the stairs, Zeta turned to look behind him. His head was level with the floor of the corridor. He saw the wheelchair shooting towards him. In horror, he reached for his gun. He raised his arm to fire. But it was too late.

The policeman fell to the floor as the wheelchair took off from the top step. It shot through the air and flew at Zeta's head. It struck him in the mouth. Both he and the chair smashed into the railings and flipped over the top. They fell with a crash and clattered to the stairs below. His gun flew into the wall with a deafening shot. It fired into the seat of the chair. A bullet ripped through it and into Zeta's back. Both man and wheelchair thudded onto the bottom step. The wheels spun with a whir, but Zeta lay still.

The policeman looked over the rail. "That'll teach you. You're under arrest."

But it was too late for that now. Zeta was dead.

*

"Can I come back to see you tomorrow?" Lee asked Georgi. "If they let me."

"I hope so," he said. "You're a brave boy. I'd like to know how you got into all this. I want to hear about my brother, too. You were one of the last people he spoke to. I want to tell you how that message we sent will change things for the better. My country will be a safer place. The bad men on that list will now be exposed for being killers back home. You'd make a good secret agent, Lee!"

They shook hands.

The policeman carried Lee to the lift. "It's just as well I let you in, young man," he said. "You took a mad risk, but you saved Georgi's life. But I'm afraid you need to know the bad news. Your wheelchair is a wreck. It's all bent. But don't worry – they're getting you a smart new one. Top of the range. A James Bond model!"

"Cool!" Lee grinned. "But I'd like to keep my old one to show people. Proof of the day I became a spy and saved the world. Well, I saved Georgi at least."

By the time he'd finished talking to the police, Lee's mum was pulling into the car park. She was bound to make a fuss that he still hadn't seen the physio yet. She'd probably get in another of her bad moods.

"Hi, love. How did you get on?" She got out of the car with a wave. "Did you cope?"

"I think so, Mum. Rather well, I think."

"Look at the state of your jeans! You look a mess. Where's your silly red cap?"

"It got shot."

"Don't be stupid, Lee. You watch too many spy DVDs. And where's your chair?"

"That got shot too. They've given me an upgrade." He laughed and pointed at his new wheelchair. "I spy with my little eye something beginning with M.O.W."

"M.O.W.?"

"Yeah, 'Meals on Wheels'. I fancy a bag of chips in my new turbo-charged spy machine!"

"Come on then. I'll treat you to chips and a pizza. I just got you another treat, too. A new DVD. It's about a boy who's a spy. A bit far-fetched… as if that could really happen."

"Thanks, Mum. Cool! You seem in a good mood all of a sudden."

She giggled. "Do you know – I can't believe my luck. I just went in to pay the gas bill. They said someone had already paid it. In cash. The garage said the same about my car bill. They must have made a mistake, but I wasn't going to argue. So shh, don't tell a soul!"

Lee smiled. "I won't say a word." And he meant it. He'd become skilled at keeping secrets… and an expert at escape. Escape from feeling a victim… and from being no more than a sitting target.

THE END